For Asia, (aka Joanna)—
my inspiration
~EL

Til Daniel og
Hannah fra Tante Jane
~JM

Published in the United States 2003
by Dial Books for Young Readers ✳ A division of Penguin Putnam Inc.
345 Hudson Street, New York, New York 10014

Published in Great Britain 2003 by Little Tiger Press
Adapted from *It's Mine!* by Ewa Lipniacka, illustrated by Basia Bogdanowiz
Crocodile Books, USA ✳ An imprint of Interlink Publishing Group, Inc. 1993

Text copyright © 1992, 2003 by Ewa Lipniacka
Illustrations copyright © 2003 by Jane Massey
Manufactured in Malaysia
1 3 5 7 9 10 8 6 4 2

Library of Congress Cataloging-in-Publication Data
Lipniacka, Ewa.
Who shares? / Ewa Lipniacka ; illustrated by Jane Massey.
p.   cm.
Published under the title: It's Mine! London : Little Tiger Press, 2003.
Summary: Two rabbits, a brother and sister, have trouble sharing what
they should, and not sharing what they should not.
ISBN 0-8037-2889-1
[1. Sharing—Fiction. 2. Brothers and sisters—Fiction.
3. Rabbits—Fiction.] I. Massey, Jane, ill. II. Title.
PZ7.L6643 Wh 2003   [E]—dc21

WHO SHARES?

Story playfully adapted from Ewa Lipniacka's It's Mine!

Ewa Lipniacka   Jane Massey

Dial Books for Young Readers 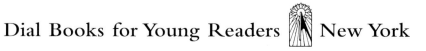 New York

"It's mine!" yelled Jack.

"Mine!" screamed Georgina.

"Oh! Now it's broken
and it's nobody's," said Mom.
"Can't you two learn to share?"

In the garden Georgina shared
her favorite worm with Jack.

And Jack shared his biggest
mud pies with Georgina.

Jack shared Georgina's
teddy bear with the dog.

And Georgina shared Jack's pencils
with the children next door.

At dinner Jack shared
his peas with Georgina.

And Georgina shared
her dinner with the cat.

Georgina shared her
bath with Jack.

And Jack shared his scariest
bedtime story with Georgina.

They both tried to
share Georgina's bed.

Then Jack began to scratch
and itch and scritch and scratch.

"Chicken pox," said Mom,
and put him to bed.

And then Georgina began to scratch
and itch and scritch and scratch.

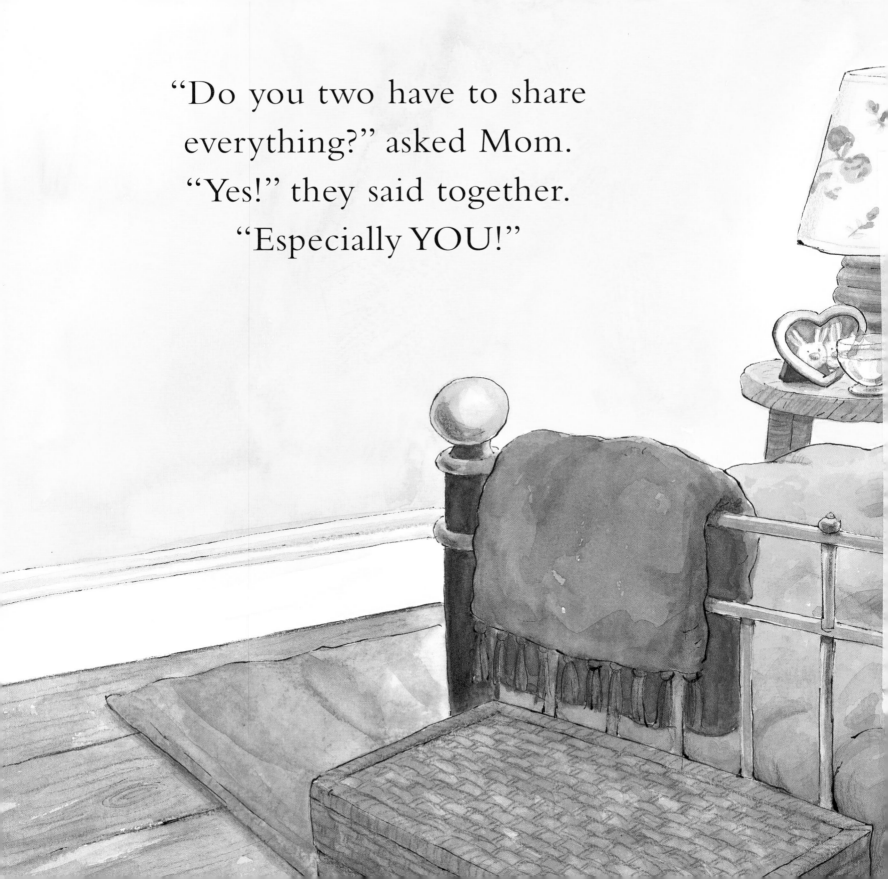

"Do you two have to share
everything?" asked Mom.
"Yes!" they said together.
"Especially YOU!"